REDUCTION IN FORCE

STEVE SOULT

REDUCTION IN FORCE

G IL RETURNED TO HIS CUBICLE after getting his morning cup of coffee. Just as he started working on a high-priority mechanical design issue, his phone rang. It was his boss. He picked it up and answered, "Hi Skipp. What's up?"

"Gil, please come to my office. I must speak to you about something quite important."

"I'll be right there." He hung up the phone and thought, *This is not good. A call from the boss on Friday usually means working through the weekend.*

He sighed, got up from his chair, and left his cubicle. It only took him about a minute to get to Skipp's office.

When Gil reached his glass-walled office, Skipp waved for him to come inside. When Gil stepped inside, he said, "Please close the door, Gil."

Gil closed the door and sat down in front of Skipp's desk. There was a blue folder in the center of the desk and a white piece of paper sitting next to it. His name, Gilbert Schaffer, was on the cover. A tight knot formed in Gil's stomach.

Skipp avoided direct eye contact with him. He nervously touched the folder with his hand. "Well, Gil, I suppose that I should cut to the chase here. As you know, our division has not met its goals for the past two quarters. Therefore, the Company has decided to cut our division's headcount by 10%. As a result of this decision, our department has been affected."

Gil's stomach cramped and he felt nauseous. He took a couple of deep breaths and asked, "So — am I one of the ones affected?"

"Yes, I'm afraid that you are."

Gil began to perspire. "Why? I have met all of our major project milestones and have had excellent appraisals. Our Mechanical Engineering design team received an award for excellence last year. It doesn't seem to me that I would be a candidate for a layoff."

"I understand that, and realize that you have been an excellent engineer." Skipp sighed and lightly drummed his fingers on his desk. "However, there were other factors involved in the Company's decision."

Gil pulled his handkerchief from his pocket and wiped the perspiration from his forehead. His hand was shaking. "Um ... what other factors?"

"Well, an important factor in the Company's decision is that it will be much less expensive to use a modern state-of-the-art AI system for our mechanical designs. This system will eliminate the need for a team of human mechanical engineers. Since you are one of our Senior Mechanical Engineers ..."

Gil interrupted, "But, there is no way that an AI system can do what our team can do! Don't they realize that?"

"Gil, *please* understand that this was not *my* decision."

Gil's voice shook as he asked, "Isn't there anything that you can do?"

Skipp shrugged and gestured helplessly. "Gil, I have known you for a long time and we have been through a lot together. Please understand that I did everything possible at my level to save your job." His voice was strained. "Unfortunately, this decision was made at the corporate level."

Skipp nervously picked up the white piece of paper, pointed to the package, and cleared his throat. "This is your separation package. After our meeting, you will be escorted to HR, where an HR representative will walk you through the contents of the package. You will not be allowed to return to your cubicle at this time. Next week you can call the office and arrange to pack up your personal belongings and take them home. Do you have any questions?"

Gil shook his head.

"All right."

Skipp picked up his phone and dialed an extension. "Barbara, this is Skipp, we are ready for you. Could you come by and escort Gil to HR, please?" He nodded and continued, "Good, we shall expect you in a few minutes. Thanks."

Skipp turned his chair away from Gil and stared silently out his window.

When Barbara arrived, Skipp handed her Gil's separation package.

Skipp looked at Gil and forced a smile. "Good luck to you, Gil. You know what they say, 'Everything will work out for the best.'"

"I sure hope that you're right."

They shook hands.

Barbara motioned towards the door. "All right, if you will follow me, we will proceed to my office downstairs."

When they arrived at her office, she invited Gil to sit down. He sat down and she settled into her black high-backed executive chair. She plopped his separation package down on her desk, and opened it.

Barbara smiled tightly and asked, "Do you have any questions before we get started?"

Nervously, Gil asked, "I am curious to know how many other people were affected by the layoff?"

"At our San Jose site, there was a 10% Reduction in Force. There is a list of the ages of the affected employees included in the back of your package. In order to show that the Company has not discriminated against employees with respect to age, the list has been sorted by age. Do you have any other questions?"

"No, not really."

"Alright, let's get started. I will walk you through the contents of your separation package and ask you to sign some documents."

Barbara pulled out the first document from the package. "In order for you to receive your separation benefits, you must agree to not work for a direct competitor for a period of one year after your separation." She turned the document around and slid it forward for him to see. "Please sign this document to acknowledge that you agree with this requirement."

Gil felt a sense of outrage at this requirement. It was bad enough that an AI system had just taken his job, but restricting his job search to non-competitive companies seemed completely unreasonable.

"What if I don't agree?"

"Then you will forfeit the separation benefits provided by the Company, which I might add, are quite generous."

Gil thought about this for a moment and then realized that the Company could not possibly enforce this requirement. He leafed through the pages of the document. It was in fine print, and to read through it would have taken at least an hour. Even then, with all of the legal terminology used, it was clear that he would not fully understand it. Only a lawyer, well-versed in corporate law, would understand all of the intricate details.

Gil pulled out a black pen, with the Company's logo on it, from his pocket protector. Flipping to the last page, he signed his name and dated it.

So much for that, he thought. *Twelve years of dedicated service all down the drain.*

Barbara countersigned the document. "Good. Let us proceed."

She walked him through the rest of the documents in the package. The separation amount was generous, and was based upon a mathematical formula that took into consideration his current salary, years of service, and earned vacation time.

The last document in the package was a list of the ages of the employees affected by the layoff. The ages were sorted in descending order. Although the list was intended to show that age was not a factor in determining who was laid off, it was apparent that most of the employees affected were older than him. He saw only two ages in their early thirties on the list. One of the ages was his: 34.

He scowled and said, "It looks to me that the vast majority of the employees laid off were older than I am."

Barbara took the list from him and frowned. "Hmm — you are right, that *is* interesting,"

Maybe they thought that they could prevent former employees from filing a class action lawsuit, Gil thought. *However, this data would support an age discrimination case, rather than discourage it.*

Barbara forced a smile and asked, "Do you have any additional questions before I call Security to escort you from the building?"

Gil wondered if he should bring up the class action lawsuit idea, but then thought better of it. "No, not at this time."

Barbara called an extension. "Curt, this is Barbara in HR. We are ready for you." She nodded. "All right, we will see you in a few minutes. Thanks."

"Security will come by and escort you from the building." She looked at her computer screen and entered her password to unlock it. "If you don't mind, while we are waiting, I have some work to do."

Gil thought that her lack of consideration for his feelings was completely uncalled-for and rude. "That's all right. I'm sure that this is a very *busy* time for you," he replied sarcastically.

"That it is, that it is ..." she replied absentmindedly as she typed on her keyboard.

While they were waiting, Gil began to feel quite anxious about the high-priority mechanical design issue that he had been working on. Then, with a sudden shock, he realized that he would never have an opportunity to fix it.

Gil wondered how an AI system could take over his job without any sort of knowledge transfer. There were countless design-related details that he carried around in his head. In addition, there was his overall vision for the product design. As he thought about this, and the long hard hours that he had spent on the project, a lump formed in his throat and his eyes misted over.

When Curt arrived, Barbara picked up Gil's separation package and said, "Curt, I need to make some copies. Please keep an eye on Mr. Schaffer until I return. I'll be right back."

"Will do," he replied bluntly.

Curt was a large burly man. *He was not the type of person that one would want to pick a fight with,* Gil thought.

After Barbara returned with her copies, she handed Gil his separation package. She nodded to Curt and said, "All right, please escort Mr. Schaffer out of the building."

Curt said in a monotonic voice, "If you will follow me, I will escort you out of the building. Where did you park?"

"In the back lot."

"All right." Curt jerked his thumb in the direction of the rear exit. "Let's go."

They walked in silence to the rear exit.

When they reached the door, Curt held it open for him and said politely, "Have a nice day."

As Gil passed through the door, he scowled and replied under his breath, "Thanks. You, too."

He clenched his fists and thought, *This is ridiculous! I have just been laid off. How could I possibly have a nice day?*

He strode quickly to his car.

■　　　■　　　■

When he returned to his apartment, Gil felt exhausted and emotionally drained. He turned on the TV and watched a couple of classic *Dr. Who* episodes. In these episodes, Davros, the creator of the Daleks, was intent on rebuilding the Dalek race decimated by the Movellans.

Afterwards, he changed into his pajamas and crawled into bed. He turned off the lights and stared at the dark ceiling. As his eyes adjusted to the dark, the texture in the ceiling came alive with the tiny faces of grotesque people staring at him.

Gil turned onto his side and thought about his meeting with Skipp. It kept replaying in his mind continuously. After lying awake for hours, he finally drifted off into a fitful sleep. Then the nightmare occurred.

He was in the process of optimizing a complex mechanical design. Just as he began a harmonics simulation, he heard the sound of heavy footsteps approaching. As they got louder, he could hear the whining of servomotors. He jumped out of his chair and peeked over the wall of his cubicle. A few yards away he saw a gigantic blue robot with glowing red eyes.

The robot halted when it saw him. It pointed at him and boomed in a loud, synthesized voice, "You shall be exterminated!"

A loud high-frequency noise emanated from the robot.

It's charging up!

Gil grabbed his model sailboat and ducked behind his steel file cabinet. Suddenly, a blinding blast of energy vaporized the top rail of his cubicle wall and blew a huge hole in his overhead file cabinet. Hot ash and debris from the blast filled the air.

The robot moved closer. "Resistance is futile!" it boomed.

The robot charged up again. The next blast blew a hole in the cubicle wall next to him. Had it not been for the file cabinet, he would have been vaporized.

Gil put down the sailboat and flattened himself against the carpeted floor. He covered his head with his arms. The robot started charging again.

"Please don't kill me. I didn't do anything!" he cried.

Another blast occurred.

Gil snapped awake, gasping for breath. He was shaking and covered with sweat. Rolling out of bed, he turned on the lights, and hurried to the kitchen.

He filled a glass halfway with ice and poured Diet Coke into it. Pressing the cold glass against his forehead he thought, *What is wrong with me? What in the world was that all about?*

Since it was early morning, he decided to stay awake, rather than going back to sleep. He did not want to re-enter *that* nightmare again.

Going into the living room, he turned on the TV. *Sleepless in Seattle* was playing on a classic movie channel. As Gil watched it, he wished that he had a girlfriend like Annie; he could really use a friend right now.

Around breakfast time, Gil thought, *My stomach feels awful — but I suppose that I should eat something.*

Gil found a slightly stale slice of raisin bread and spread some peanut butter on it. He took a bite and walked over to his computer desk. With some trepidation, he opened his separation package.

Well, let's see what we have here.

In addition to the copy of the papers that he had signed yesterday, he found a color brochure, and a thin spiral-bound book in the package. They were intended to make the transition to being unemployed easier.

Gil opened the brochure and flipped through it. It provided information about a Silicon Valley foundation that provided assistance to the unemployed.

On the glossy cover of the book was a picture of an attractive blonde woman dressed in a dark business suit. She was talking to a man who had been laid off. Her office was flooded with golden sunlight streaming through the office window. The title, "Making the Adjustment", was set in an ebullient and optimistic typeface.

Gil opened the book and read the first part of the introduction, which briefly described the five stages of grief:

1. Denial
2. Depression
3. Anger
4. Bargaining
5. Acceptance

I wonder if I am in the denial stage?

When Skipp told him that he was laid off, it felt like he had fallen into an abyss. He felt disoriented and could not process his termination details. When he went to HR, he still felt disoriented and could not focus on what Barbara told him.

At lunchtime, Gil still did not feel hungry, so he turned on the sports channel. The Giants were scheduled to play the Diamondbacks that afternoon.

When the game started, he slid his Ultra HD 3-D VR headset over his eyes and immersed himself in the game at Chase Field. The Giants lost the game in extra innings.

After the game he thought, *I suppose that I should eat something. Maybe a bowl of soup would be good.*

Gil went into the kitchen and made a cup of tomato soup. He picked up the cup, went over to his computer desk, and turned on his computer. While sipping the soup, he reviewed the skills section of his resume.

What good are my skills compared to an AI system? There is no way that I can compete with it. It is accurate, cheaper, and faster. It never sleeps, never gets sick, and never takes a vacation.

After trying to revise his skills section — and not making any progress — Gil realized that he would have to completely rewrite his resume.

Gil applied for his unemployment benefits and calculated how long his funds would last. He only had enough for about six months. After that, he would have to start liquidating his retirement account assets.

He put on his pajamas and crawled into bed. After tossing and turning for a couple of hours, he finally drifted off into a restless sleep. In the early morning, he had another nightmare.

This nightmare started like the first one. In this version, the robot — which he decided to call the "Exterminator" — blasted away some other cubicles on the aisle. Rather than wait for it to blast his cubicle to bits, Gil decided to make a break for it. Since it took a few seconds for it to recharge, he decided to wait until the next blast and then flee while it was recharging.

Gil grabbed his sailboat and hid behind his file cabinet again. Then, after the next blast, he charged out of his cubicle, and raced down the aisle away from the Exterminator.

The Exterminator boomed, "You shall be exterminated!"

Gil heard it charging up. He ducked into the last cubicle on the aisle.

The next blast blew the manager's glass-walled office at the end of the aisle to bits. Smoking debris and hot shards of glass flew everywhere.

Gil sprang up, dashed out of the cubicle, and sprinted towards the door to the first-floor stairway. He flung open the door and quickly ran down the stairs.

When he reached the first floor, he burst through the door and ran across the parking lot. The next blast blew a huge hole through the side of the building. Smoldering debris scattered all over the parking lot. He could see the Exterminator's glowing red eyes glaring at him through the hole.

"Resistance is futile!" Its loud booming voice echoed across the parking lot.

He heard it charging up.

I need to get out of here!

Gil forced himself to wake up. He was out of breath, hot, and sweaty.

After rolling out of bed and turning on the lights, he stumbled to the kitchen. After putting some ice in a glass, Gil filled it with water, and then splashed some lemonade in it.

Sipping it slowly he thought, *At least I wasn't exterminated. However, if it keeps this up, I'm not going to get much sleep.*

Gil entered the living room and turned on the TV. The first episode of *The Prisoner* was playing on a classics TV channel. In this episode, Number Six tried to escape by the beach outside of the Village, but was incapacitated by Rover.

At breakfast time, he discovered a hard-boiled egg hiding behind a mustard jar in the refrigerator. After making a cup of coffee, he nibbled on the egg and turned on his computer.

Gil decided that understanding his nightmares had a much higher priority than searching for a job. He spent most of the day doing research on nightmares. Evidently, altering the outcome of a nightmare was the correct approach. He decided to see what else he could do if the nightmare reoccurred.

At dinnertime, Gil found a frozen burrito in the bottom of the freezer and heated it up in the microwave. He carried it over to his computer desk and, while it was cooling, started a brand-new resume. The skills section was still a problem, so he focused on his work history, listing his projects in reverse chronological order.

After going to bed, he stayed awake, considering various alternatives to deal with the Exterminator. It seemed like running away had worked well, but what he really needed to do was to defeat it. After an hour or so, he came up with an idea. Confident that it might work, he drifted into sleep. As before, the nightmare reoccurred in the early morning.

In this version of the nightmare, he went downstairs to the lab and fabricated a large concave shield from silica tiles and applied a mirror-like surface. He thought that if he could reflect the Exterminator's blast it would have a disastrous effect.

This time, when he heard the Exterminator blasting away the nearby cubicles, he took the shield, went into the aisle, and placed it in position.

When the Exterminator saw him, it boomed, "You shall be exterminated!"

Gil yelled, "I don't think so!"

The Exterminator started charging up. Gil knelt down behind his shield, being careful to cover his entire body, and braced himself for the blast.

The blast hit the shield with tremendous force. Despite the incredible heat from the blast, his shield held. Abruptly, the blast ended.

He peered over the top of his shield to see what had happened.

The reflected blast had wiped out the entire right side of the robot's torso. Its eyes were dimming and it tottered back and forth.

In a slow, quavering voice it said, "Resistance .. "

It fell over on its side with a tremendous crash.

Gil dropped his shield, walked over, and kicked it. The Exterminator was dead.

He woke up.

■　　■　　■

After breakfast he called Skipp's number to schedule a time to pick up his stuff. When there was no answer, he left a message. After another hour, he called again. Once more there was no answer, so he left another message.

Gil anxiously waited for another hour. After the hour was up, he decided that Skipp was not going to return his calls. He then called their secretary, Marisa, to see if she could help.

Marisa was able to give him a 20-minute time slot at 4:40 PM the next day.

■　　■　　■

He arrived at the Company's site about 20 minutes early and went into the main lobby. The receptionist was on the phone. She motioned for him to wait and continued talking.

After a few minutes of emotional conversation, she slammed down the phone. She had tears in her eyes, and, in a broken voice, she asked, "Good afternoon. May I help you?"

"Yes, my name is Gilbert Schaffer, and I have a 4:40 appointment with my manager, Skipp Larson, to pick up my things. I was laid off last Friday."

She made an effort to regain her composure. "Okay, let me see if Mr. Larson is ready for you."

She dialed his extension but there was no reply. She left a message for him.

She pointed to the couch in the lobby. "Have a seat over there, please. He should return my call shortly."

In a few minutes, her phone rang. She answered and nodded her head. "All right, that will be fine."

She looked at Gil and said, "I'm sorry, Mr. Larson will not be able to see you today. He has a very important meeting to attend."

"What!" Gil replied angrily.

The guy lays me off and then doesn't even have the common decency to help me pick up my stuff. What does he think I am supposed to do?

"So, what am I supposed to do?"

The secretary cringed and picked up her pen. "Um ..." She clicked her pen nervously. "He asked me to contact Security and have them escort you to your cubicle."

"Oh ... great."

She called Security and after about ten minutes, Curt came into the lobby. He looked at Gil, grunted, and then pointed in the direction of the stairs. He escorted Gil to his cubicle without saying a word. When they got to his cubicle, Curt posted himself at the door.

Gil entered his cubicle and quickly looked around to make sure that everything was still there. The only thing that was missing was his computer. They had taken it away, leaving a tangled mess of cables on the floor.

Marisa came by with an empty copy paper box. "Here is a box for you, Gil. How are you doing?"

"All right, I guess."

"That's good. Denise wanted to see you as soon as you got in."

"She did?"

"Yeah, I'll go get her."

"Okay, thanks."

Denise was the Project Manager for the Sierra project. He had known her since she first joined the Company five years ago. She was honest, direct, and didn't hesitate to speak her mind. This put her at odds with many of the other engineering managers.

She probably wants to discuss some of the Sierra project details, he thought. *After all, there was absolutely no opportunity for a smooth transition of my design work to the AI system.*

He began packing his possessions carefully one-by-one. He wished that he had some bubble wrap and another box for his model sailboat. It had taken him over 80 hours to build it. He was looking for something to wrap it with when Denise stepped around Curt and entered his cubicle.

"Lady, you are not allowed in here," Curt growled.

She turned and glared at him. "Look here, Mister, I am the PM for the Sierra project, and I have some very important things to discuss with Mr. Schaffer." She put her hands on her hips and took a step towards him. "Since what we need to discuss is confidential, I must ask you to leave. I will escort him out of the building when we are done."

Curt had a stunned expression on his face. He shrugged and gave a mock salute. "Yes Ma'am!"

He did an about-face and marched away.

Denise looked at Gil with a concerned expression. "How are you doing, Gil? You look really tired."

"Well to be honest, I haven't been sleeping well. I've been having nightmares. They have been pretty difficult to deal with."

"That's understandable, after what you have been through." She pushed up her glasses and looked at him closely.

"Yeah, I suppose."

He looked into her eyes and his shyness suddenly got the better of him. Denise was very attractive. She was about 5' 5" and thin, but with an athletic build. Her long dark brown hair cascaded over her shoulders. The bangs along her forehead just touched the top of her glasses, which magnified her large cobalt blue eyes. Spending time outdoors had given her a lightly tanned complexion.

"Um ... I suppose ... um, that you're here to discuss the Sierra project," he stammered.

She looked disappointed. "No, not really. We were informed this morning that the Sierra project is in danger of being canceled."

Gil was flabbergasted. "Oh no! Really?"

"Yes. If the new AI engineering technology doesn't pan out, or if we don't meet the Corporation's newly revised milestones, the project will be canceled."

"But they've spent millions of dollars on it! They can't do that!"

She sighed and replied, "They can do anything that they want to do."

"I'm sorry, Denise. That's awful."

She pushed her hair back, tilted her head slightly to one side, and looked at him. "Actually, I wanted to see how *you* were doing." She moved closer and touched his arm.

"You did?"

"Yes."

"Oh ..."

She smiled and said, "Here, let me help you pack the rest of your stuff."

It didn't take long for them to pack the rest of his things. Finally, only the model sailboat was left.

"Denise, you wouldn't happen to have some bubble wrap and another box, would you?"

"No, but Marisa can get it for us. Here, let me call her."

After she spoke to Marisa, she picked up the model and studied it. "This is a really beautiful blue water cutter, Gil. The workmanship is outstanding, and every detail is absolutely correct."

"Thanks," he replied, pleasantly surprised. "I spent a very long time on it. Its best feature is that you can actually sail it by remote control. The antenna is incorporated into the mast."

"You can! That's wonderful!" She laughed and said, "I love to sail, too!"

"You do?"

"Absolutely! I learned how to sail when I was a little kid. I was born and raised in Stratford, Connecticut, you know. My family has a seafaring history spanning several generations."

"That's great! I had no idea."

Suddenly, the thought of asking her out flashed through his mind.

Then he lost his nerve.

She wouldn't be interested in me. I'm unemployed with no current job prospects and, besides, she probably wouldn't want to sail a model sailboat. She's an expert sailor.

She wrapped the model and carefully packed it in the box.

"Well, I suppose we should get you out of here."

"Say, Denise, I was thinking that maybe ..." he panicked and couldn't finish the sentence.

"Hum?" She looked at him with a puzzled expression.

"Um ... I was wondering if you would like to keep the model. You know, as sort of a remembrance."

She gasped and smiled broadly. "Are you sure, Gil? You must have spent at least a hundred hours on it."

"Yeah, I'm sure. I'd really like you to have it."

"Oh my ... I would really love to have it. But, if I accept it, I have one condition."

Gil felt very apprehensive. "What's that?"

"That we go out and sail it together sometime."

Gil gave a sigh of relief. "Of course ... sure, I'd really like to do that."

She extended her hand. "Shake on it?"

"Okay." He grinned and shook her hand.

"All right! Stay *right here*. I'm going to go and hide it under my desk. I'll be right back!"

She picked up the box, looked around carefully to make sure that no one was watching, and quickly walked away. In a few minutes, she returned.

She said breathlessly, "Okay, let's go!"

He picked up his box and Denise escorted him downstairs to the main lobby.

When they reached the lobby, she took her cell phone out of her pocket and waved it. "Do you have my cell number?"

"No, sorry, I just have your work number."

"All right, what's yours?"

As he gave her his number, she tapped it into her phone.

His cell phone rang. He put his box down, pulled his phone out of his pocket, and answered, "Hi, Denise."

"Hi, Gil." She laughed. "Now, you have my number."

"Right, thanks!"

"Don't forget to call me."

"I won't!"

She went over to the front door and opened it for him. Gil picked up his box and passed through the door. After it slammed shut, he strode quickly across the parking lot to his car.

■　　　■　　　■

When Gil returned to his apartment, he felt exhausted. He didn't feel like cooking, so he grabbed a half-empty bag of potato chips, went into the living room, and turned on the TV to watch the news.

The news was awful and it made Gil feel extremely depressed. It seemed like society was in a steep decline. After scanning through the channels, and not finding anything good to watch, he turned off the TV.

Then he decided to turn on his computer and read his email; a large amount of it was junk. After a couple of hours, he decided to go to bed.

That night, Gil had a different nightmare. He was in a foreign country standing by himself on a village street. In the far distance, he could hear the sound of surf breaking on the shore.

It was dusk, and the sky was blanketed with dark gloomy clouds. The buildings were shut and there was no one else to be seen. He checked his pockets and they were empty: no phone, no passport, no wallet, and no keys. Gil was lost, penniless, and alone.

Suddenly, the wind picked up and it began to rain. The rain was bitterly cold. It began to rain harder and soon his clothes were drenched. He started to shiver and desperately looked for shelter.

A large ledge hung over the doorway of one of the buildings, close to where he was standing. He ran over to it and sat on the doorstep, partially protected from the deluge. Anxiously, he looked up and down the street for someone to help. It was empty.

All of a sudden, a huge bolt of lightning struck the top of the roof of a building across from him. It showered the street with smoldering debris. The building caught on fire. Before long, it was completely engulfed in flames. Smoke and steam from the fire billowed into the sky.

Desperate and unsure of what to do next, Gil woke up. His heart was pounding, and he felt cold and clammy. After he got out of bed, he turned on the lights, and slogged to the kitchen. After heating up a cup of water in the microwave, he added a chamomile teabag.

Great! I just exterminated the Exterminator and now I have to deal with being lost. I don't have anything in this nightmare; no office, no lab, and nothing in my pockets. What am I supposed to do?

After a few minutes, Gil added a lemon slice and some honey to the tea. After taking a sip, he went over to his desk and turned on his computer.

He spent the rest of the morning researching nightmares. For those who have suffered a trauma, nightmares are quite common. This explained why he was having them. He came to the conclusion that the best interpretation of last night's nightmare was a literal one: he was completely lost.

At lunchtime he ate a peanut butter sandwich and wrestled with the prospect of calling Denise. He wanted to call her, but now after this nightmare, he was reluctant to. If he told her about it, she would probably think that he was crazy. He finally decided to send her a text message instead.

He pulled out his phone and hesitated. He took a couple of deep breaths and thought, *Okay, you can do this. Just go ahead and invite her out to lunch.*

He took another deep breath and texted: *Lunch tomorrow?*
After a short delay she replied. *Sure, where and when?*
Giuseppe's at Noon?
Great! See you then!
At the end of her text, she had added a smiling face emoji.

■   ■   ■

When he arrived at the restaurant, she was waiting inside for him. As he entered, she stood up to greet him.

She smiled and said, "Hi, Gil. How are you doing?"

He didn't know if he should tell her the truth or just give an innocuous reply. "Okay, I guess."

She looked at him with a concerned expression. "You look pretty tired. Are you all right?"

He wiped his brow with his hand. "I'm ... well, I'm dealing with something. Maybe we should talk about it."

She looked worried. "All right, that would be fine."

The *maître d'* greeted them and smiled, "Sir, do you have a reservation?"

Gil replied, "Yes, I am Gilbert Schaffer and I have a reservation for two for lunch."

The *maître d'* checked his list of reservations and said, "Welcome Mr. Schaffer. Please follow me."

The maître d escorted them to a table for two with a nice view of the city's busy downtown area. After they were seated, Denise pushed her glasses up and asked in a strained voice, "So, what did you want to talk about, Gil?"

"You're probably going to think that I am crazy, but I've been having some terrible nightmares."

"I know. You mentioned it before."

He described the Exterminator nightmares and how he finally resolved them. Then, very hesitantly, he described his latest nightmare, which he decided to call the "Village" nightmare. He told her that he didn't have a solution for it. He paused and waited for her to reply.

She thought about it for a while. "Well, you know how you introduced the shield in the last Exterminator nightmare?"

"Yeah."

"Well, maybe you can introduce something useful into the Village nightmare."

"Okay, like what?"

She laughed and said, "For one thing, you really need an umbrella. Maybe you can bring one with you or find one somewhere."

"That's a really good idea. I hadn't thought of that."

"The other thing is, I figure that the rain is going to put out the fire. You just have to stay away from it so that you don't get burned. It's like ... well, like how you escaped from the Exterminator."

These suggestions made him feel much better. He decided to give them a try.

After they finished their lunch, Denise had to get back to work. Before she left, they agreed to get together for lunch at Giuseppe's every Wednesday. This would be something for him to look forward to.

When they parted, she gave him a quick hug. "Take care and, if you need to talk to someone, don't hesitate to call me."

"Okay, I'll do that. I really appreciate your help, Denise. Thanks."

"Sure, don't mention it." As she left, she gave a quick wave.

Gil grinned and waved back.

■   ■   ■

During the next few weeks, Gil focused on finding a new job. He set a target of submitting five resumes per day. Since each version of his resume had to be tailored to a specific job description, this amounted to nearly a full day's work.

The Village nightmare persisted. He tried introducing items — such as Denise's umbrella, for example — into the nightmare. Although this helped, it did not end the nightmares. It seemed that every time he solved a problem, another one would present itself.

After two months, Denise expressed her concern about the deterioration of both his physical and mental condition.

After they sat down at their table at Giuseppe's, she looked at him sadly and said, "You know, Gil, you aren't doing so well."

This made him feel angry. "What do you mean?"

"I mean ... well, you are not taking care of yourself, you have lost a lot of weight, and you are extremely emotional."

He scowled and replied, "I'm doing the best that I can!"

"I know that — but maybe you should seek some professional help."

"Like what? See a shrink or something?"

"Maybe. I have been doing some research on Post-Traumatic Stress Disorder — PTSD. Many people who have been laid off suffer from it."

Gil was shocked.

"Really?" he replied angrily.

"Yes, that's right." She sighed, took off her glasses, and wiped her eyes. "I'm only trying to help you, Gil."

"By sending me to a shrink?"

"That is for you to decide." She put her glasses back on and said, "Did you know that they can treat PTSD now by removing memories? Here, I have something for you." She reached into her purse, pulled out some papers that were stapled together, and handed them to him.

He took the papers and his heart sank.

She was supposed to be his friend. Couldn't she be supportive?

She looked at him and said seriously, "Gil, will you promise me something?"

"Maybe ... it depends."

"Promise me that you will follow up on this. I just don't want to be involved with someone with PTSD."

"What?"

"Will you *please* get some help?"

He stared at her.

She said sadly, "I have to get back. Please let me know what you decide."

She got up, grabbed her purse, and left the restaurant.

■   ■   ■

That night, the Village nightmare was worse. He had lost the items that he had accumulated, and the intensity of the fire was worse than ever. He snapped awake with feelings of despair and absolute abandonment.

After breakfast, Gil studied the papers that Denise had given him. The papers contained information about PTSD and the new treatment based upon erasing memories. There was also information about some of the leading practitioners in the field. He went online to look up treatment success rates and to find the best local practitioner.

Denise is right. I have to do something about this!

Gil called the University Medical Center and scheduled a consultation with Dr. Harold Barnes, an expert in treating PTSD by erasing memories.

■   ■   ■

Gil called Denise right after he made his appointment.

"Hi, Gil," she answered.

"I did it, Denise."

"Oh ... did what?"

"I made an appointment with Dr. Barnes."

She said happily, "That is really great news, Gil!"

"I was wondering if you could go with me to the appointment?"

"Um, when is it?"

"Next Thursday at 10 AM."

"Let me check my calendar."

"Ah, if you're busy, it's okay."

"No ... I want to go. How about I meet you there?"

"That would be great. Thanks!"

■　　　■　　　■

Dr. Harold Barnes was in his mid-fifties, tall and lanky, with short gray hair. After introducing himself, he gave Gil a firm handshake.

He looked at Denise and asked, "And, you are Mrs. Schaffer?"

Denise blushed. "Um ... no, I'm Denise Martin. Gil is a former co-worker of mine."

"Oh, sorry ... it's just ... well, no matter. Will you be taking Mr. Schaffer to the hospital for treatment?"

"Yes."

"Good. That is quite important. After treatment, many patients experience dizziness or other symptoms that will impair their ability to drive safely."

"I understand. I will keep a close eye on him."

"Good."

Dr. Barnes then described the risks, the procedure, and what to expect. After he was done, he asked them if they had any questions. They shook their heads.

He asked Gil to step out of the room so that he could talk to Denise privately.

When she came out of the room, Gil asked her, "What was that all about?"

Denise gave him a furtive glance. "Oh, nothing, really."

She looked worried.

■　　　■　　　■

On the treatment day Denise picked him up and drove him to the hospital. They arrived about forty-five minutes before his appointment. She had allocated extra time to find a parking place and get to the neurological treatment section of the hospital.

When they got to the waiting room, Denise looked very nervous. "Gil, I hope that your treatment goes well. I … I feel like I pushed you into this."

"It's okay. I'm sure that it will be fine," he replied nervously.

About fifteen minutes after Gil's scheduled time, a nurse opened the waiting room door and called his name. After he went through the door, she smiled and said, "Good morning Mr. Schaffer, I am Minh Nguyen and I will be helping you today. How are you?"

"Actually, I feel quite nervous."

She said, "Please try to relax, we will take good care of you."

"Okay, thanks."

She took him to a dressing area. It had a privacy curtain and was just large enough to accommodate a hospital bed. There was a steel chair and a cabinet that could be locked. On top of the cabinet was a neatly folded hospital gown, a pair of blue shorts, and a plastic bag.

"Mr. Schaffer, are you wearing dentures, do you have any implants, or have a pacemaker?"

"No."

"Good. All right, please take off your clothes and put the shorts and gown on. If you are wearing any metal objects, please remove them and put them in the plastic bag. You can also put your phone, keys, change, and wallet in the bag. Do you have any questions?"

"No."

"If you need help, I will be right outside." Minh closed the privacy curtain of the dressing area with a loud swoosh.

Gil put the items from his pockets into the plastic bag. Then, he took off his clothes and put them on the cabinet. Shivering, he put on the shorts and unfolded the hospital gown. He slid the gown over his arms and fumbled with the ties on the back of the gown.

After a couple of minutes, Minh asked from outside the curtain, "Do you need some help?"

"Yes, please."

"May I come in?"

"Yes."

She slid open the curtain partway and entered. With a few deft motions of her hands, she tied the gown securely behind Gil's back.

She pointed to his left arm and said, "Please don't forget to put your watch in the plastic bag."

"Oh ... right."

He took off his watch and put it into the bag. She locked the bag inside the cabinet.

"Good, please wait until they are ready." She opened the privacy curtain and walked away.

A short time later, she returned. "You will go to Diagnostics now. The technician there will do your scan."

He got up and followed Minh to the Diagnostics room. Adjacent to the room was an operator's area with an observation window. The doorway to the operator's area was open.

A huge medical scanner stood in the center of the room. A narrow, padded table ran on a track into its throat.

A technician wearing a green hospital uniform greeted Gil. "Hello, Mr. Schaffer, I am Brian Plummer and I will be conducting your scan today."

Gil felt uneasy. He pointed to the throat of the scanner. "Will my head be going in there?"

"Yes. First, we must perform a complete scan of your brain. Then, we will identify the specific location of the memories that you want erased."

Gil nervously ran his hand through his hair. "Will it hurt?"

"No, but you may experience a slight feeling of warmth and see some bright flashes of light. This is normal and nothing to be concerned about."

Gil got up on the table and laid down. His stomach knotted and he felt nauseous.

"Please put your arms next to your body and try to relax." Brian instructed.

Brian gave Gil a panic button to hold in his hand. "You can press this button at any time to stop the scan. However, please do not do it unless it is absolutely necessary."

"Okay." He clutched the panic button and tried to remain calm.

"All right, Mr. Schaffer, I will go into the operator's area now. There is an intercom system there so I will be able to hear you and provide any additional instructions. All right?"

"Okay."

A little while later, Brian's voice came over the intercom, "Mr. Schaffer, I am now going to initiate the full scan of your brain. Please relax, breathe slowly and steadily, and remain still. Are you ready?"

Gil closed his eyes tightly and replied, "I guess so."

The table moved forward slowly until the top of Gil's head was close to the throat of the scanner. The scanner then turned on with a loud *clunk*. A loud, whining noise emanated from it, reminding him of the Exterminator. The noise increased in pitch until it reached a steady-state level.

Gil felt very uncomfortable and the loud scanner noise was terrible. As his head entered the throat of the scanner, he felt a slight momentary vibration and heard a faint grinding noise.

It has a bad bearing, he thought.

When his head was partway into the scanner, stars formed in front of his eyes. He gasped, pressed the panic button, and yelled, "Stop it! I'm seeing stars! It's going to fry my brain!"

The table stopped moving. Brian said, "Please remain still, Mr. Schaffer. What you are experiencing is normal. The scan will not hurt your brain. You are not in any danger."

Gil gasped and tried to calm himself. "All right ... sorry."

The table moved back a little and then moved forward again. This time, when Gil began to see stars, he forced himself to take slow steady breaths until the scan was completed.

"Good, you may breathe normally again," Brian said. "Please remain still while we reset your head position."

The table moved Gil's head back to its original position.

"Mr. Schaffer, we will now identify the specific areas of your brain associated with the memory that you want erased. You must concentrate on the specific memory that you want erased. It is *absolutely essential* that you concentrate fully on that — and only that — memory. Under no circumstances should you let your mind wander, as this may cause problems later with your treatment. Do you understand?"

"Problems? What sort of problems?"

"The success of your treatment is based upon the accuracy of your memory scan data. If your memory scan data includes areas outside of the specific memory area, then those areas will be erased as well during your treatment."

"That sounds really bad."

"It can be." Brian paused and then asked him, "Are you ready?"

Gil closed his eyes tightly again and replied, "I guess so."

"All right, we will now begin your memory scan. Please breathe slowly and steadily and remain still during the scan."

As before, the table moved slowly until the top of his head was near the scanner's throat. Then, the scanner turned on again with a loud *clunk* and started generating the loud whining noise again. As before, the sound made Gil feel very uncomfortable.

"Mr. Schaffer, I want you to now focus completely on the memory that you want erased. Do not let your mind wander, all right?"

"Okay," Gil mumbled.

The table moved Gil's head into the throat of the scanner. He focused on the intense memory of his meeting with Skipp, triggering a flood of negative emotions. Suddenly, he felt a slight vibration and heard a faint grinding noise. It broke his concentration, shifting his focus momentarily away from the memory. Before he could refocus on it, the scan ended.

"All right, we're done," Brian's said cheerfully over the intercom. He came out of the operator's room and helped Gil get off the table. Minh came in moments later and said, "I will take you to Treatment now."

■　　　■　　　■

The Treatment room was smaller than the scanner room. A large padded chair sat in the middle of the room. Dangling from the chair were restraining straps clearly designed to hold the patient's arms and legs in position.

A steel table stood next to the right side of the chair. A transparent helmet was sitting on top of the table. It had a large array of electrodes sticking out of it. Wires from the electrodes, bundled together into a harness, traveled up to the ceiling and then over to a computer system.

Gil looked at the helmet and thought, *Oh no! It looks like a modern version of Doc Brown's brain-wave analyzer. I sure hope that it works!*

On the left side of the chair stood an IV stand with an infusion pump mounted on it. A bag of fluid hung from the stand. Gil saw other pieces of complex medical equipment in the room that he did not recognize.

Dr. Barnes and another doctor were waiting for him. Dr. Barnes introduced the other doctor, who was an Anesthesiologist.

Dr. Barnes said, "Mr. Schaffer, we will now put you to sleep for your treatment. Do you have any questions before we begin?"

I wonder if I should tell him about my attention wandering during the scan?

He decided not to mention it. "No, not really."

"Good, please sit down and we will get started."

Gil cautiously eased himself into the chair and Minh strapped him in. The straps on his arms and legs were very tight and uncomfortable. The Anesthesiologist deftly inserted an IV into his arm. He connected the line to the pump and turned it on. After the Anesthesiologist injected a drug into the line, Gil fell into a deep sleep.

When he woke up, the restraining straps and the IV had been removed. His body ached all over and he had a splitting headache. Minh was standing next to him with a concerned expression on her face.

"I will tell Dr. Barnes that you are awake." She went away and, in a few minutes, returned with him.

Dr. Barnes checked Gil's pupils and discussed his aches and pains with him. He prescribed some pain medication that Gil could take on an as-needed basis.

Minh helped him get out of the chair. When Gil stood up, he felt dizzy. He sat down again and rubbed his face.

"Are you all right, Mr. Schaffer?"

He waved her away and said, "Just give me a minute or two."

Soon, the dizziness subsided, and he stood up.

Minh escorted him back to the dressing area. She unlocked the cabinet for him, closed the privacy curtain, and waited for him to put his clothes back on.

After he was dressed, she escorted him back to the waiting room.

When Denise saw Gil come through the door, she rushed over to him and gave him a gentle hug. "How did it go?"

"All right, I guess." He stepped back and stared at her. "Say, Denise, I thought that you had shorter hair."

"Oh, no," Denise moaned. "Dr. Barnes had warned me about this!"

"About what?"

"That you might not remember anything about *us*. You know, about our lunches together, our conversations, and everything." Tears welled up in her eyes.

"Denise, please don't worry, I do remember it. It's just ... well, I am really confused right now. You had much shorter hair at work."

"Oh, I *see*." She gave a sigh of relief. "I did, but that was a long time ago."

After they picked up his prescription, they drove back to his apartment. Gil began to realize that they had wiped out much more of his work-related memory than he had anticipated. He had forgotten virtually everything about the Sierra project and his last two years at the Company. However, he could remember most of the details of his personal life outside of the Company — which included sailing his models.

■   ■   ■

Although Dr. Barnes had said that there would be a gradual improvement in his memory, after a couple of weeks he still could not remember any work-related details for the past two years.

Perhaps this is a good thing, Gil thought. *Actually, I don't feel too bad about this. But, on the other hand, I can't remember anything about my computer system or how to use the mechanical design software that I listed on my resume.*

His cell phone rang. It was Denise.

"Hi, Gil, how are you doing?"

"Pretty good."

"Are you still having nightmares?"

"No, not really."

"That's wonderful! How about your memory?"

"It seems like I can't remember anything work-related for the last couple of years."

"That's great!"

"Well, maybe... I can't remember using the latest software tools listed on my resume. That will be a real problem during a job interview."

"Oh, ... may I offer a suggestion?"

"Sure."

"You should think outside the box."

"Outside the box?"

"Yeah, maybe you should take this opportunity to do something that you have always wanted to do."

"Do you have something in mind?"

"Well, actually I do. Do you remember the model of the blue water cutter that you gave me?"

"Of course."

"I can assume that, since you know so much about sailboats, you are an experienced sailor."

"Um ... no, not really. I've sailed the models, of course. But, I've never sailed a *real* sailboat."

"Really?"

"Yeah, I hate to admit it, but I've never taken sailing lessons."

"Well, I can teach you how to sail. What do you think?"

"That's a terrific idea!"

"Wonderful! Are you free next Saturday?"

"Sure."

"All right, how about I pick you up at 8:30 AM."

"Okay, that sounds really good. Do I need to bring anything?"

"Wear jeans and sneakers. Since we will be sailing on the Bay, a sweatshirt won't do much good. I recommend that you bring a turtleneck, a wool sweater, and a windbreaker. You should also bring a knit cap. It can get cold and really windy."

"Okay, I have some old tennis shoes, a sweater, and a windbreaker. But, I don't have a turtleneck or a knit cap."

"What size are you?"

"I think that I'm a Large now."

"I'll see if I can get something for you."

"Thanks! Oh, by the way, I was wondering what type of sailboat you have?"

"Actually, I'm thinking about purchasing a used Tayana 37. However, I can borrow a sloop from a family in the club. I taught their kids how to sail and they are really good friends of mine."

"That sounds great!"

After he hung up, Gil felt happier than he had ever remembered.

■　　■　　■

On Saturday morning Denise arrived right on time.

She handed Gil a navy blue turtleneck and a matching knit cap. "Here, I got these for you. It might get chilly on the Bay today."

Denise drove north on 101 to the Peninsula Avenue turnoff, went to the Coyote Point Marina, and parked near one of the docks. When Gil got out of the car, he saw a bewildering array of sailboats moored there.

Far beyond the marina he could see white-capped waves riding on the Bay. *Oh no, it looks pretty rough out there!*

Denise opened the door to the dock with her key. They walked quickly down to where a sloop was moored. Her name, *Annastasia*, was painted in ornate gold letters on her stern and she was in absolutely pristine condition.

Denise said, "All right, Gil, get on board!"

He stepped on board, lost his balance when *Annastasia* rocked, and quickly sat down.

Denise laughed, cast off the lines, and then nimbly hopped on board. Soon, they were underway.

When *Annastasia* reached the Bay, the offshore wind filled her sails and she heeled over. She picked up speed and sliced through the waves effortlessly.

After sailing for a few miles, Denise handed Gil the tiller. She showed him how to tack and jibe, and taught him some of the finer points of sailing. It was the most exhilarating experience of his life.

When they returned to the dock late in the afternoon, Gil felt very sad.

"What's wrong, Gil?"

"It's just that ... well, I just wish that we could have sailed longer."

She grinned and replied, "So do I."

"Say, Denise, I was wondering if I could take you out to dinner."

"Are you sure?"

"It is the least that I could do to repay you. Besides, it would be a perfect ending to a perfect day."

"That would be really nice. Do you like seafood?"

"I do."

"Good! There's an excellent restaurant here on the Point. We could go there."

"Sure, that sounds wonderful."

They drove the short distance to the restaurant and were quickly seated. They started with glasses of chardonnay, followed by calamari, and then the best halibut that Gil had ever tasted. When they finished eating, they ordered glasses of port wine.

Gil held his glass up and said, "To a perfect day."

They clinked glasses.

"Yes, to a perfect day."

Denise took a sip of port and quickly put her glass down. She looked troubled.

"Is there something wrong?"

"Um, I didn't want to bring it up, but ..."

"Go ahead, please tell me, Denise ..."

She sighed and said, "Well, they decided to cancel the Sierra project yesterday. That means that I am a PM without a project."

"Oh no! I'm *so* sorry!"

She ran her fingers through her hair and tried to smile. "It's okay, really. I wasn't planning to work there much longer."

"What are you going to do?"

"Um, well ... I suppose that I am going to have to think outside the box." She took another sip of her port and looked at him. "Gil,

I was wondering if maybe, um … maybe you would like to sail to Maui with me?"

Gil was dumbfounded.

Seeing the expression on his face, Denise shook her head. "It's okay, I understand. It's an absolutely crazy idea…"

"I'll do it."

She looked astonished. "What?"

"I'll do it."

"You will?"

"Of course!"

She jumped up, rushed over, and kissed him gently.

Sometimes, Gil thought, smiling to himself, *things do work out for the best.*

ABOUT THE AUTHOR

Steve Soult graduated with a BS EE degree from the University of Santa Clara. He then went to the Navy's OCS in Newport, RI and was commissioned as a US Naval Officer. During the Vietnam War, he was stationed at the Great Lakes Naval Base. After his release from active duty, he attended the University of California at Berkeley on the GI Bill, earned an MS EECS degree, and was hired by IBM in San Jose.

While at IBM, Steve received an Outstanding Technical Achievement Award and had an article published in the *IBM Journal of Research and Development*. IBM also paid the tuition for his MBA degree in Management from the University of Santa Clara. IBM began to downsize its operations in Silicon Valley after Steve had worked there for over 17 years. After surviving several rounds of layoffs, he decided to leave IBM and join Abbott Laboratories.

Steve retired from Abbott Laboratories to pursue his lifelong interests in art, photography, and writing full time. He has three grown children who are all employed as engineers in Silicon Valley. He lives in Morgan Hill with his wife, Susanne, and his dog, Snowy.